JAMES

PERCY

MEET ALL THESE FRIENDS IN BUZZ BOOKS:

Thomas the Tank Engine
The Animals of Farthing Wood
Biker Mice from Mars
Winnie-the-Pooh
Fireman Sam
Rupert
Babar

First published in Great Britain 1991 by Buzz Books
an imprint of Reed Children's Books
Michelin House, 81 Fulham Road, London SW3 6RB
and Auckland, Melbourne, Singapore and Toronto
Reprinted 1993 (twice), 1995

ISBN 1 85591 151 5

Printed and bound in Italy by Olivotto

POP GOES
THE DIESEL

buzz books

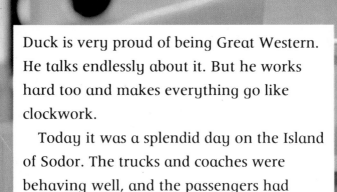

Duck is very proud of being Great Western. He talks endlessly about it. But he works hard too and makes everything go like clockwork.

Today it was a splendid day on the Island of Sodor. The trucks and coaches were behaving well, and the passengers had stopped grumbling! But the engines didn't like having to bustle about.

"There are two ways of doing things," Duck told them. "The Great Western way, or the wrong way. I'm Great Western and . . ."

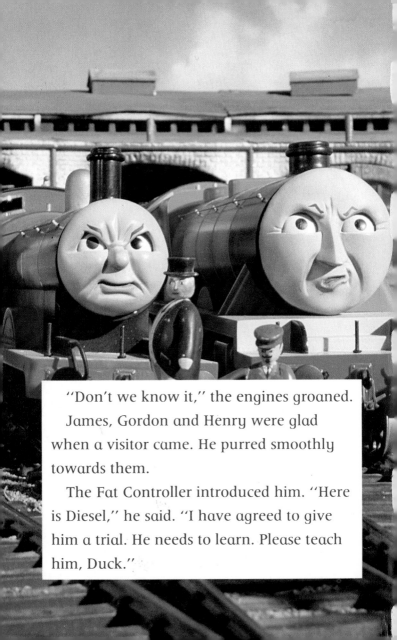

"Don't we know it," the engines groaned.

James, Gordon and Henry were glad when a visitor came. He purred smoothly towards them.

The Fat Controller introduced him. "Here is Diesel," he said. "I have agreed to give him a trial. He needs to learn. Please teach him, Duck."

"Good morning," purred Diesel in an oily voice. "Pleased to meet you, Duck. Is that James – *and* Henry – *and* Gordon, too? I am delighted to meet such famous engines."

The silly engines were flattered. "He has very good manners," they murmured to each other. "We are very pleased to have him in our yard."

Duck had his doubts. "Come on," he said, impatiently.

"Ah yes!" said Diesel. "The yard, of course. Excuse me, engines."

Diesel purred after Duck, talking hard. "Your worthy Fat . . ."

"Sir Topham Hatt to you," ordered Duck.

Diesel looked hurt. "Your worthy Sir Topham Hatt thinks I need to learn. He is mistaken. We diesels don't need to learn. We know everything. We come to a yard and improve it. We are revolutionary."

"Oh!" said Duck. "If you're revo-thingummy, perhaps you would collect my trucks while I fetch Gordon's coaches."

Diesel, delighted to show off, purred away.

When Duck returned Diesel was trying to take some trucks from a siding. They were old and empty. They had not been touched for a long time. Diesel found them hard to move.

Pull – push – backwards – forwards.

"Oheeer! Oheeer!" the trucks groaned. "We can't! We won't!"

Duck watched with interest.

Diesel lost patience. "GrrRRRrrrRRR!" he roared, and gave a great heave. The trucks jerked forward.

"Oh! Oh!" they screamed. "We can't! We *won't*!" Some of their brakes snapped and the gear jammed in the sleepers.

"GrrRRRrrrRRR!" roared Diesel.

"Ho! Ho! Ho!" chuckled Duck.

Diesel recovered and tried to push the trucks back, but they wouldn't move.

14

Duck ran quietly round to collect the other trucks. "Thank you for arranging these, Diesel," he said. "I must go now."

"Don't you want this lot?" asked Diesel.

"No, thank you," replied Duck.

Diesel gulped. "And I've taken all this trouble," he almost shrieked. "Why didn't you tell me?"

"You never asked me. Besides," said
Duck, innocently, "you were having such
fun being revo-whatever-it-was-you-said.
Goodbye."

Diesel had to help the workmen clear the
mess. He hated it. All the trucks were
laughing and singing at him.

"Trucks are waiting in the yard;
  tackling them with ease'll
'Show the world what I can do,'
  gaily boasts the diesel.
In and out he creeps about,
  like a big black weasel.
When he pulls the wrong trucks out
  - Pop goes the Diesel!"

17

The song grew louder and louder and
soon it echoed through the yard.

"Grrr!" growled Diesel and scuttled away
to sulk in the shed.

DIRTY WORK

buzz books

When Duck returned, and heard the trucks singing, he was horrified. "Shut up!" he ordered and bumped them hard. "I'm sorry our trucks were rude to you, Diesel," he said.

Diesel was still furious. "It's all your fault. You made them laugh at me."

"Nonsense," said Henry, "Duck would never do that. We engines have our differences;' but we *never* talk about them to the trucks. That would be des – des . . ."

"Disgraceful!" said Gordon.

"Disgusting!" put in James.

"Despicable!" finished Henry.

Diesel hated Duck. He wanted him to be sent away. So he made a plan. He was going to tell lies about Duck.

Next day he spoke to the trucks. "I see you like jokes. You made a good joke about me yesterday. I laughed and laughed. Duck told me one about Gordon. I'll whisper it . . . don't tell Gordon I told you," said Diesel and he sniggered away.

"Haw! Haw! Haw!" guffawed the trucks. "Gordon will be cross with Duck when he knows. Let's tell him and pay Duck back for bumping us."

They laughed rudely at the engines as
they went by. Soon Gordon, Henry and
James found out why.

"Disgraceful!" said Gordon.

"Disgusting!" said James.

"Despicable!" said Henry. "We cannot
allow it."

They consulted together. "Yes," they said,
"he did it to us. We'll do it to him, and see
how *he* likes it."

23

Duck was tired. The trucks had been cheeky and troublesome. He wanted a rest in the shed.

But the engines barred his way. "Hooooosh! KEEP OUT!" they hissed.

"Stop fooling," said Duck, "I'm tired."

"So are we," said the engines. "We are tired of *you*. We like Diesel. We don't like you. You tell tales about us to the trucks."

"I don't."

"You do."

"I don't."

"You do."

The Fat Controller came to stop the noise.

"Duck called me a 'galloping sausage'," spluttered Gordon.

". . . rusty red scrap iron," hissed James.

". . . I'm 'old square wheels'," fumed Henry.

"Well, Duck?" said the Fat Controller, trying not to laugh himself.

Duck considered. "I only wish, sir," he said gravely, "that I'd thought of those names myself. If the dome fits . . ."

"He made the trucks laugh at us," said the engines.

"Did you, Duck?" asked the Fat Controller.

"Certainly not, sir. No *steam* engine would be as mean as that."

Diesel lurked up. "Now, Diesel, you heard what Duck said," said the Fat Controller.

"I can't understand it, sir," said Diesel. "To think that Duck of all engines . . . I'm dreadfully grieved, sir, but I know nothing."

"I see," said the Fat Controller. Diesel squirmed and hoped he didn't.

"I'm sorry, Duck," said the Fat Controller, "but you must go to Edward's station for a while. I know he will be glad to see you."